Just the Way You Are

By Kara McMahon
Illustrated by Joe Mathieu

Creative Edge, 2009. All rights reserved.
Published by Creative Edge, 2009, an imprint of Dalmatian Press, LLC, Franklin, Tennessee 37067. No part of this book may be reproduced or copied in any form without written permission from the copyright owner. 1-866-815-8696

Printed in the U.S.A.
ISBN: 1-40378-815-4

09 10 11 NGS 10 9 8 7 6 5 4 3 2 1
CE11642 Sesame Street 8x8 Storybook: Just the Way You Are

"See you next week, Miss Linda!" Zoe called as she left dance class. She twirled and leaped down the street. Class might have ended, but Zoe still felt like dancing!

"I love being a ballerina," she said happily.

Whoosh! Flash! Swoosh!
"Super-Duper Elmo to the rescue!" Elmo cried.

"I don't need to be rescued!" Zoe said with a giggle. "But I do need to practice my ballet steps. Do you want to practice with me?"

"Well, Elmo *was* playing superhero . . . ," said Elmo, "but okay. Elmo can try to practice ballet."

"Ballet dancers don't usually wear capes," Zoe explained. "So you should take off that cape."

"Watch this," Zoe instructed. She turned gracefully. "Now you try."
Elmo tried to copy Zoe, but he almost lost his balance.

"Nice try," Zoe said. "Try this instead." She leaped gracefully and landed softly.

Elmo took a running start and leaped through the air yelling, "Super-Duper Elmo!" He landed with a big thud.

"No, Elmo, that's not right!" Zoe said.

"Sorry, Zoe, but Elmo doesn't like ballet as much as you do," Elmo said. "Let's play superheroes instead, okay?"

Zoe could not believe her ears. Elmo said he didn't really like ballet! But Zoe was a ballerina. And if Elmo did not like ballet, that must mean that Elmo did not like ballerinas. Did that mean that Elmo did not like *Zoe*?

Elmo put his cape back on. "Do you have a cape you can wear?" he asked.
"Sorry, Elmo, I have to go home now," Zoe said, rushing off.
"Wait, Zoe!" Elmo called after her. "You can pretend your tutu is a cape!"
But Zoe was gone.

Zoe walked slowly down the street. She did not feel proud and happy. Instead she felt sad.

Zoe tugged on her tutu. "I really want Elmo to like me," she said to herself. "So if Elmo doesn't like ballet, then that means I can't be a ballerina anymore."

Zoe walked over to the nearest trash can. Should she throw away her beloved tutu?

"Hey, don't bother me during lunch!" a grouchy voice grumbled.

"Oh, sorry, Oscar," Zoe replied. "I didn't realize this was your can. I was just thinking about throwing away my tutu."

"This *tutu* is *too, too* nice to be trash!" Oscar said, scowling. "Why would you want to throw it away?"

"My tutu *is* trash," Zoe said sadly. "I don't want it anymore. Maybe you can use it for something."

Oscar scratched his head. *Well, if Zoe doesn't want it anymore, then I guess it <u>is</u> trash,* he thought.

But what could a grouch do with a tutu?
Oscar tried dangling it outside his can
as a trashy flag, but it looked too pretty.

He tried wearing it as a hat,
but it just wasn't grouchy enough.

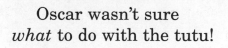

Oscar wasn't sure
what to do with the tutu!

"Super-Duper Elmo is looking for Zoe," Elmo called as he walked by Oscar's can. "Hey, why does Oscar have Zoe's tutu?"

"It's not a tutu anymore," Oscar answered from inside his can. "It's trash!"

"This tutu is way too nice to be trash!" Elmo declared. "May Elmo have it, please?"

"Too nice? I knew it! Yuck!" Oscar popped up out of his can. "Take it! Zoe went that way. Now SCRAM!"

Elmo ran to find Zoe. "Super-Duper Elmo rescued Zoe's tutu from Oscar,"
he called as he ran up to his friend.

"Elmo, I *gave* the tutu to Oscar," Zoe said. "I don't want it anymore."

"But you *love* ballet!" Elmo said, sounding puzzled.

"Yes, but you don't," Zoe explained. "And since I want you to like me, I decided I can't be a ballerina anymore."

"But Elmo *does* like Zoe!" Elmo said. "Elmo likes you just the way you are!"

"Just the way I am?" Zoe asked, still unsure. "Even as a ballerina? Even though you don't like ballet as much as I do?"

"Elmo is very sorry for hurting Zoe's feelings," said Elmo, handing Zoe her tutu. "Elmo likes Ballerina Zoe. And Elmo would like Astronaut Zoe or Farmer Zoe, too."

"Okay, Elmo!" said Zoe. "Thank you for my tutu. And I'm sorry I asked you to take off your cape."

"Hey, Elmo, I have a great idea," Zoe said as she stepped into her tutu. "We can play superheroes *and* practice ballet. And I can be Super-Duper Ballerina Zoe!"

And so she was!